WARNING! DO **NOT** USE YOUR REAL NAME!

"WHAT IS WRITTEN IN BOOKS CAN BE TRUE UP TO A POINT
AND MISTAKEN UP TO A POINT. ONE MUST NEVER TRUST BOOKS
TOTALLY, INSTEAD ONE MUST CHECK WHAT IS RIGHT AND WRONG
IN THEM, AS YOU HAVE RIGHTLY DONE. I CONGRATULATE YOU
AND YOUR TEACHER ON THIS AND SEND MY WARMEST GREETINGS
AND BEST WISHES."
—ITALO CALVINO,
"LETTER TO THE PUPILS AT COLETTI MIDDLE SCHOOL,"
NOVEMBER 21, 1967
(TRANSLATED FROM THE ITALIAN BY MARTIN MCLAUGHLIN)

A NOTE ON THE ART

Certain eagle-eyed readers may notice some "discrepancies" in the colors of
objects in this book's illustrations. For instance, a red laser appears orange in the
pictures. Or a brown violin appears, in the art, to be a lovely shade of teal. A vial
of dragon's blood is black, when of course in real life dragon's blood is an eerie
green. You might see all this and think, "Hey, what gives?" Or you might not think
that, because you already know what's going on: We print these books using just
three kinds of ink: black, orange, and that teal I mentioned earlier, which, really, I
find to be such an appealing color. So in the pictures of this book, everything—no
matter what color it actually is—will appear black, orange, or (beautiful) teal. Or
white, where we didn't use any ink and you just see the page. Why did we do this?
Because we like how it looks! And we hope you do too.
—M.B.

For Greg Pizzoli
— M.B.

For Jack, Louise, T.L., and Mildred
— M.L.

Library of Congress Cataloging-in-Publication Data available
ISBN 978-1-338-59426-3
10 9 8 7 6 5 4 3 2 1   20 21 22 23 24
Printed in China   62 • First edition, September 2020
The text type was set in Twentieth Century.
The display type was hand lettered by Mike Lowery.
Book design by Doan Buu

MAC B.

KID SPY

THE SOUND OF DANGER

By **Mac Barnett**
Illustrated by **Mike Lowery**

Orchard Books
New York
An Imprint of Scholastic Inc.

ME AS A
~~KID~~
SPY!

MY NAME IS MAC BARNETT.
I AM AN AUTHOR. BUT
BEFORE I WAS AN
AUTHOR, I WAS A KID.
AND WHEN I WAS A
KID, I WAS A (SPY).

AN AUTHOR'S JOB IS TO
MAKE UP STORIES. BUT
THE STORY YOU ARE
ABOUT TO READ IS TRUE.

THIS ACTUALLY HAPPENED
TO ME.

In 1989, I looked like that.

If I look like I am stressed out in the picture, that's because I was. It was a Friday, and every Friday in 1989, my whole class had to do a Mad Minute.

A Mad Minute was a worksheet with sixty math problems. When we came back from lunch on Fridays, there would be a Mad Minute lying on each of our desks. Our teacher, Mr. M., would stand at the front of the classroom and hold up a stopwatch.

Mr. M. would wear a striped referee's shirt, because he thought that would make doing a Mad Minute fun. (It didn't.)

We would pick up our pencils.

We would hunch over our papers.

GOPHER!

Mr. M. would shout.

We weren't allowed to start when he said "gopher"—only when he said "go." He thought saying "gopher" would make doing a Mad Minute fun.

(It didn't.)

"Ha ha, got you, Tiffany!" Mr. M. would say. "On your mark. Get set . . ."

Our hearts were beating hard.

GOJI BERRY!

Some of us would sigh or groan. Tommy would always laugh, but Tommy was a kiss-up.

"Ha! All right, all right," Mr. M. would say. "For real. On your mark . . .

"Get set . . ."

GHOST HOUSE!

"Good one, Mr. M.!" someone would say, probably Tommy.

At my desk I would think, "Ghost house? That's not even a thing. It's called a haunted house."

And I would be sitting there, thinking about ghosts, when Mr. M. would say, "On-your-mark-get-set-go!" as fast as he could and click his stopwatch.

We had three minutes to solve all the problems on a Mad Minute. (Confusing name.)

If you got every answer on your worksheet right, you moved up a level, which meant that the next Friday you got a harder Mad Minute.

There was a big chart on the wall with all our names on it, and which level we were on.

There were ten levels.

I was on Level 4.

I had been stuck on Level 4 for seven weeks.

When I was a kid, I wasn't great at math.

(I'm still not.)

But I could usually get the right answer if I had enough time to think about it. The stopwatch freaked me out, and I made what Mr. M. called "careless errors."

I tried not to think about the clock and did my best to solve the math problems.

In the row next to me, Derek Lafoy leaned back in his chair like he was at the beach. "Oh yeah, baby," he said. "This is the life!"

The week before, Derek had been the first kid in our class to finish Level 10. Mr. M. had called him a "math whiz." If our teacher had called anyone else a "math whiz," Derek would have made a "whiz" joke. Instead, Derek had just tapped his temple and said, "I'm the whiz, man!"

MATH WHIZ

When you finished Level 10, Mr. M. took you to get ice cream after school, and you never had to do a Mad Minute again.

At his desk, Derek Lafoy said "Ahhhhhhh," like he had just taken a big sip of soda on a hot day.

I was having trouble multiplying eight times seven. You might know the answer. You might even be thinking, "That's easy!" But I bet nobody is holding a stopwatch in front of you right now. Derek Lafoy probably isn't sitting next to you saying, "Oh yeah, baby!"

Lucky you.

Mr. M. blew a silver whistle. It was an awful sound. "That's time!" he shouted.

I filled in all the blank problems as fast as I could.

"Pencil down, Mac!" said Mr. M. "Put that pencil down!"

I slapped my pencil on my desk and rested my chin in my hands.

"Pass your papers up to the front," said Mr. M.

Derek leaned over and looked at my worksheet. He winced. "Ooooooh," he said, shaking his head.

Mr. M. told us to read at our desks while he corrected our Mad Minutes. I pulled out my book.

But I couldn't concentrate on reading, because every few minutes, Mr. M. would ring the bell at his desk and say "Ashley! Level Nine!" or "Tommy! Level Eight!" or "Tiffany! Level Ten!" and they'd get to walk over and put a sticker on the chart.

Derek raised his hand. "Mr. M.? If I already reached Level Ten, could I go get ice cream again if I bought it with my own money?"

"No," said Mr. M.

Mr. M. marked up our sheets with a red pen.

I tried to focus on my book.

I hoped my name would get called.

And then, my name did get called.

But not by Mr. M.

The school secretary's voice came in over the intercom: "Mac Barnett, please report to the office. Mac Barnett to the office."

MAC BARNETT TO THE OFFICE.

"Oooooooooooohhhhhhhh," Derek Lafoy said. "Busted."

But I knew I wasn't in trouble. When I was a kid, I didn't get in trouble at school. I stood up and went to the office.

Mrs. Planter, the school secretary, smiled when she saw me. "Your mom is on the phone," she said. "She has to pick you up early today."

I frowned.

"But I'm supposed to go to my dad's this weekend."

Mrs. Planter shrugged. She pointed to the phone on her desk.

While I reached to pick up the receiver, Mrs. Planter said, "I didn't know your mom wasn't from here."

"What?" I said.

"She has a British accent," Mrs. Planter said. "It's so cute!"

"Oh!" I said. "Yeah. I forget sometimes, because she's my mom. She does have a cute British accent."

My mom did not have a cute British accent.

I knew then that it wasn't my mom on the phone.

It was the Queen of England.

9

"Hello?" I said.

"Hullo!" said the Queen of England. "It's me, the Queen of England!"

"I know," I said.

"Mac," said the Queen, "today I am acting like an undercover spy myself. I told the woman who picked up the phone I was your mother! So you mustn't say anything to me that you wouldn't also say to your mother. For instance, do not call me 'Your Majesty.' Unless you also call your mother 'Your Majesty.'"

"OK," I said.

"Do you call your mother 'Your Majesty'?" asked the Queen.

"No," I said.

"Well, perhaps you should. She would probably enjoy it," said the Queen. "Oh, this is so much fun! I fooled your school secretary with my American accent! Would you like to hear it?"

"OK," I said.

The Queen of England cleared her throat. "I would like to eat Doritos while I watch television all day, misterrrrrrr." She really hit the "r's" hard. It wasn't a great accent.

"That's great!" I said.

"I know!" said the Queen. "As I understand it, Doritos are a kind of corn chip. Is that right? How do you make a chip out of corn? Oh! Yes, of course, what you Americans call 'chips,' we Britons call 'crisps'! A corn crisp! But how do you make a crisp out of corn? Anyway! It is important that you come to London immediately. I have a mission for you, Mac."

"OK," I said. "Mom."

"A car shall arrive for you shortly," said the Queen of England. "Good-bye."

"Good-bye," I said.

The Queen of England sighed. "Mac, that is not how you would end a call with your mother. Come now! I will not hang up this phone until you say, 'I love you too, Mother.'"

"But—" I said.

"But nothing!" said the Queen. "Say it!"

There were a few seconds of silence.

"I love you too, Mother," I said.

Mrs. Planter, who had been pretending not to listen to my phone call, smiled sweetly.

The Queen of England made a satisfied grunt. "Good-bye!" she said, then hung up the phone.

Mrs. Planter wrote me a note, and I took it back to my classroom. I packed up my desk and gathered my things.

My backpack was extra heavy because it was full of stuff to take to my dad's:

MY GAME BOY →

MY WALKMAN ↓

A RECORDER →

A recorder is a plastic flute. At my school, they taught all the kids to play the recorder. We were supposed to bring them home in our backpacks and practice every night. My mom didn't like the sound of my recorder playing. I don't think any of our parents did. So none of us actually learned how to play the recorder. Once a year, my whole class gave a recorder concert. It was terrible.

When I got back to the office, Mrs. Planter was staring out the window.

"Wow!" she said. "I didn't know your mom drove a stretch limo."

A black limousine was parked in front of the school. There was a sign in the back window with my name on it.

The phone rang, and Mrs. Planter picked it up. "OK," she said. "OK . . . Oh, good-bye!"

Mrs. Planter hung up the phone. "Your mom said that she's here, and then she said her favorite food is corn crisps, and then she hung up on me."

I nodded. "Sounds like her," I said.

And I walked out of school.

And that is how it happens. One minute you are sitting in class, hoping a teacher wearing a referee shirt rings a bell so you can put a sticker up on a bulletin board. The next minute you are on a plane to London, on a mission for the Queen of England. The life of a spy is strange, but the life of a kid is also strange.

It takes a long time to fly to London from California. So I pulled out my Game Boy.

I played my favorite game, SPY MASTER, for a couple of hours, until I got tired of it.

Then I switched to my second favorite game, Tetris.

In Tetris, different-shaped blocks fall from the sky.

You try to arrange the blocks into a wall. If you make a line of blocks, the blocks disappear, which makes room for more blocks. The further you get, the faster the blocks fall. There are no bosses. There are no weapons. Mario is not in the game. It's just blocks, blocks, blocks.

And more blocks.

But once you start playing Tetris, it's hard to stop.

When I was a kid, I could never figure out exactly why the game was so addictive. But it must have something to do with the Tetris song.

The Tetris song started like this:

dum doo doo dum

doo doo dum

doo doo dum

doo doo dum

doo dum dum doo doo dum

(It's really hard to write a great tune using only words. Just listen yourself. You can look it up.)

All night, while I flew over the ocean, blocks fell down the screen of my Game Boy.

The Tetris song played through my headphones:

dum doo doo dum

doo doo dum

doo doo dum

doo doo dum

doo dum dum doo doo dum

Hours vanished. Time drifted by swiftly. I ordered a milk from the flight attendant, and then I ordered another. Blocks fell and disappeared and soon—

dum doo doo dum

doo doo dum

doo doo dum

doo doo dum

doo dum dum doo doo dum

—the plane touched down hard, and I was in London.

The Tetris song was still in my head as I took a taxi to Buckingham Palace.

"What is that song you're humming?" the Queen of England asked. She was sitting on her throne, in Buckingham Palace, eating the Doritos I'd brought her.

"It's the Tetris song!" I said.

"Well, please stop humming it," said the Queen of England.

I stopped.

"Now—" said the Queen.

"Wait," I said. "Before you start, there's something I've been meaning to talk to you about."

The Queen of England stared at me. She did not like being interrupted.

I pretended not to notice. "I've gone on a lot of missions for you," I said. "And I always get the job done."

"Mostly," said the Queen.

"So when do I get a code number?"

"A what?" said the Queen.

"A code number," I said. "You know, like James Bond. Agent Double O Seven!"

I struck a cool pose.

The Queen's forehead puckered. "And what do you know about James Bond?"

"He's in movies!" I said. "My mom won't let me watch them because she says there's too much romance."

"He is also in books," said the Queen. "Mac, James Bond is a fictional character. You are a real kid, and an actual spy. Her Majesty's Secret Service—excuse me, *My Majesty's* Secret Service—does not really assign code numbers to spies."

"Oh," I said. "OK."

"Now—" said the Queen.

"But I'd still like one," I said.

The Queen of England stared at me again.

"You'd still like *what*?" said the Queen.

"A code number," I said. "They sound cool!"

"Very well," said the Queen.

I pumped my fist.

"You can be . . ."

The Queen munched a chip.

"One," said the Queen of England.

"*One*?" I said. "That sounds dumb."

The Queen of England shrugged. "I told you, we don't give spies numbers. So you're the first. One."

"Aw man." I was glum. "Agent One . . ."

"Now," said the Queen of England. "You must listen closely, Agent One, and stop interrupting me. I have a mission for you. And this mission involves tremendous violence."

I gasped!

5

TREMENDOUS VIOLENCE

"Why did you just gasp?" asked the Queen of England.

"Sorry. I didn't mean to interrupt you."

"A gasp does not count as an interruption," said the Queen. "I am just confused about why you are gasping."

"Because," I said. "You just said this mission involves tremendous violence!"

The Queen of England frowned.

"No," she said. "I said it involves tremendous *violins*."

"Ohhh," I said. "I get it. Please, go ahead."

The Queen of England grunted, then continued. "As I was saying," she said, "this case involves tremendous violins. The best in the world. I assume you know what a Stradivarius is—"

"Let me just interrupt you right there," I said. "I don't."

The Queen of England stared at me.

She kept staring at me for a long time.

A really long time.

8

THE MISSION
CONTINUES!

TOP
SECRET!

Finally, she sighed.

"What are they teaching you children in America?"

"Right now, Mr. M. is really focused on Mad Minutes."

"I have no idea what that means," said the Queen, "but unfortunately, I am sure you will tell me."

"We have to do a bunch of math problems in three minutes."

"Then why is it called a Mad Minute?" the Queen asked.

"I know," I said. "I told Mr. M. at the beginning of the year that it wasn't a good name. But he said nobody cared what I thought about names. Then later, after class, he apologized for snapping at me, but I think he was just afraid that I would tell my mom what he said, and then she'd call and leave him an angry phone message again."

"Even though that story did not have an ending, I hope it is over," said the Queen of England. "Because now it is time for me to tell you a story. And this is not a story about math. It is a story about music! Three hundred forty-five years ago—"

"Oh boy," I said.

ANTONIO STRADIVARI

"Three hundred forty-five years ago," said the Queen of England, "in a tiny town in Italy called Cremona, a boy named Antonio Stradivari was born. He would grow up to become the greatest luthier to ever live!"

I smiled.

The Queen looked at me carefully. "You do not know what a luthier is, do you?"

"Nope!" I said.

"A luthier makes stringed instruments. And the strings are my favorite part of the orchestra. So much more beautiful than percussion, so much finer than the brass. Now—"

"You forgot about the woodwinds," I said.

The Queen of England frowned. "Excuse me?"

"There are four parts of an orchestra," I said. "Percussion, brass, strings, and woodwinds. Like flutes. Or the recorder! I play the recorder!" I pulled out my recorder. "Want to hear 'Mary Had a Little Lamb'?"

"I do not," said the Queen. "Please put that away. And do not ever tell me I forgot about the woodwinds. That is a very rude thing to say."

"OK," I said.

"I won't stand for it," she said.

"OK," I said.

"Absolutely unacceptable," said the Queen.

"Now. Stradivari loved violins. And people loved the way Stradivari's violins sounded. Soon he was famous! He made violins for kings and queens, barons and bankers. Stradivari made hundreds of violins in his life, and he signed every one of them with his name:

Stradivarius

"I thought you said his name was Stradivari," I said.

"Well, he signed them with his name in Latin," said the Queen.

"Why in the world would he do that?"

"Panache," said the Queen. "You wouldn't understand."

"Hmmm," I said.

"Today, a Stradivarius can sell for more than 645,000 pounds!"

"How much is that in dollars?" I asked.

"About one million dollars," said the Queen of England.

"You should just say it in dollars," I said. "It sounds more impressive!"

The Queen frowned at me.

I pretended not to notice. "Why are they so expensive?" I asked.

(Today, in 2020, when I am writing this book, Stradivarius violins are even more expensive. One sold for 16 million dollars, or 12.3 million pounds, which sounds less impressive.)

"Because," said the Queen of England, "Stradivari's violins sound better than any other."

"What's so great about them?"

"Their *tone*," said the Queen. "Do you know what tone is?"

"Mmm, yes," I said. "Sometimes when I get smart

with my mom, she says she doesn't like my tone."

"Precisely!" The Queen clapped her hands. "The tone of your voice makes your words sound bad! But the tone of a Stradivarius makes music sound wonderful. As much as your mom dislikes your tone, that is how much people *love* the tone of a Stradivarius."

"Why do they sound so good?"

"If we knew how to make a violin sound like a Stradivarius," said the Queen, "every violin would sound like a Stradivarius. Some people think it's because he only used wood from trees in which nightingales sang. Some people say it was because he coated the wood with a special varnish to protect it. A mixture of sap and spice and dragon's blood.

"But most people think Stradivari's violins are the best simply because he was very good at making violins. Today, only five hundred of Stradivari's violins survive. Each one has its own name."

"Good names?" I asked.

"Wonderful names!" said the Queen. "These are the names of the top five Stradivarius violins:

"Good names," I said.

"Indeed," said the Queen. "And each violin has its own personality."

"Like the New Kids on the Block?" I said.

"The what who on the where?" said the Queen of England.

JOEY   DANNY   JORDAN   DONNIE   JONATHAN

"They're a boy band," I said. "Derek Lafoy says the New Kids are really lame. And he makes fun of anyone who likes them. And I guess I see his point, but they sing that 'The Right Stuff' song, and it's actually pretty good!"

(That's true. You can look it up.)

"Seriously. Listen to it. It's actually pretty good!" I said.

"Please," said the Queen, "do not tell me what I should do. I am a queen, and you are a boy. An American boy."

"Sorry," I said.

"Now," asked the Queen, "why would violins be like a boy band?"

"Each one has a different personality," I said. "The nice one, the cute one, the shy one, the older brother, and the bad boy."

"Ah," said the Queen. "Then yes, exactly like the New Kids on the Block."

THE SHY ONE

THE BAD BOY

THE OLDER BROTHER

THE NICE ONE

THE CUTE ONE

THE LADY BLUNT

THE MESSIAH

THE LADY TENNANT

THE CREMONESE

THE VIOTTI

"And," said the Queen of England, "each Stradivarius has its own story. For instance, the Viotti. It is named after Giovanni Viotti.

GIOVANNI VIOTTI

"He was born in 1755 to a poor blacksmith. But he was so wonderful at playing violin that he traveled across Europe to perform at royal courts! The Empress of Russia gave him a Stradivarius.

CATHERINE THE GREAT

"He took it to Paris, where he became the personal musician to the Queen of France!

MARIE ANTOINETTE

GULP!

"But in 1789 things in France began to go wild. There was a revolution! And in 1793 they cut off the queen's head."

"That's awful," I said.

"Imagine how I feel," said the Queen of England. "Soon after that, the French began cutting off lots of people's heads, and Giovanni, who needed his head to play violin, packed up his Stradivarius and fled to England. Very sensible."

"OK," I said.

"But when Giovanni died, his Stradivarius returned to France." The Queen rolled her eyes. "The Viotti got passed from hand to hand, from collector to collector, until the Bruces, who are a lovely family, bought the Viotti so that it could remain in Britain forever."

"OK," I said. "That's a nice story."

"It's not over," said the Queen of England. "Last night, the Viotti was stolen!"

"No!" I said.

"Yes!" said the Queen. "And listen to this! Two nights ago, the Lady Tennant was taken from its owner. And the night before that, someone burgled the Lady Blunt! Notice a pattern?"

"Somebody is stealing the top five Stradivariuses!" I cried. "Stradivarii? That doesn't sound right . . ."

"You may just call them Strads," said the Queen.

"Someone is stealing the top five Strads!" I cried.

"Correct!" said the Queen.

"Who do you think is taking them?" I asked. "The KGB Man?"

HEE
HEE
HEE

The KGB Man was my archenemy. He was a spy for the Soviet Union. He caused chaos. He played tricks. And, one time, he had stolen my blue jeans.

He still hadn't given them back.

"Why," said the Queen of England, "do you always think it is going to be the KGB Man?"

"Because it always is!" I said.

"Not always," said the Queen.

She had a point.

"Well, usually!" I said.

"Mac," said the Queen, "not every mission is going to be some Cold War plot."

When I was a kid, adults were always talking about the Cold War—on the news, at dinner, in the movies. I knew we were in a cold war with the Soviet Union, but I didn't really know what a cold war was.

"Your Majesty," I said. "Can I ask you something? Why is it called 'the Cold War'?"

"Come now," said the Queen. "Why do you think?"

"Because in Russia," I said, "it's really cold?"

"No!" said the Queen. "The Cold War is called a cold war because it is not fought with bullets." She pointed to her head. "The Cold War is fought up here as well. It is about which side has better spies. Which side has better stories. Which side has better ideas."

"OK," I said.

"But why are we talking about this? My point is that this has nothing to do with Russia, the Cold War, or the KGB Man!"

"OK," I said.

"In fact, I think I know who took the violin. I just need you to prove me right."

"Hmmm," I said.

"It just so happens that the Messiah, perhaps the finest Strad of them all, is also here in England. And if this pattern continues, tonight is your chance to catch the thief red-handed!"

This is Oxford University.

It is a very good school. They even have a museum! The museum at Oxford is named the Ashmolean Museum, because it started with a collection of stuff owned by a man named Elias Ashmole.

(Wow. What a name.)

Here is some of the stuff Elias Ashmole gave to the museum:

a jester's uniform (real),

REAL ↓

a phoenix wing (fake),

FAKE →

and a stuffed dodo (real).

Today, more than three hundred years later, they have a bunch more stuff:

a samurai suit,

some mummies,

and a painting of a naked baby playing what looks like a violin, while riding a dolphin.

(The dodo is still there.)

By the time I got to the museum, it was closing down for the day. A curator showed me around. She seemed annoyed I was there.

"Our alarm system is state of the art," she said. "Guards have checked the whole building. There is nobody hiding in the air vents, or the mop closets, or the toilets. You and I are the only ones left in the museum."

"OK," I said.

"This is a quiet place. The only mystery afoot is that this morning somebody took four rolls of toilet paper from the men's room on floor two."

"Interesting," I said.

"Not really," said the curator. "You would be surprised how often it happens. Every three weeks, at least. We always say it must be someone who needs it more than we do."

We walked toward the exit.

"This museum is secure," said the curator. "Once I lock the front door, nobody will be able to get inside without setting off bells. Robbing it would be completely impossible."

"I've heard that before," I said.

Now she seemed even more annoyed.

"And so I would rather you leave the museum when I do," she said. "It is a bit odd to let somebody spend the night in a museum."

I shrugged. "I just do what the Queen of England tells me to do."

The curator sighed. "Well, I guess I do too. Good night. Please don't touch anything."

She walked out the door. Her keys jangled. Many locks clicked.

I was alone in the museum.

I went to go see the Messiah.

It was in the middle of a gallery under a glass case. A light shone down on the case from above.

It looked like an ordinary violin.

"Huh," I said to myself. "I guess it must sound nice."

My voice bounced around the empty room.

I began my patrol of the museum.

When I was a kid, I really wanted to spend the night in a museum. But when I imagined spending the night in a museum, I always pictured sleeping there, in the fancy bed of some ancient king.

When I *actually* spent the night in a museum, it was my job to stay awake the whole time, walking around, guarding a violin.

I walked from gallery to gallery. I hummed a little tune to myself because when I was in a quiet place, I would get lonely.

(I still do.)

After a few hours, it was very dark outside, and I got tired and bored.

I went to a café and called the Queen of England on a pay phone.

"Hullo, Agent One," said the Queen.

"Aw man," I said.

"I am glad you called," said the Queen. "I have been wanting to scold you. That song you told me about has been stuck in my head ever since we spoke this morning."

"The New Kids on the Block song?" I said. "It's actually pretty good, right?"

"No," said the Queen. "The one that goes:
dum doo doo dum
doo doo dum
doo doo dum"

"Oh!" I said. "The Tetris song. I was just humming it too! It's catchy, right?"

"It's terrible," said the Queen of England. "I haven't been able to concentrate on the book I am reading, and I was just getting to an exciting part."

"Well, things are pretty quiet around here," I said. "Maybe I should call it a night and get some sleep."

"Don't be ridiculous!" said the Queen. "When things are very quiet, that is how you know something exciting is going to happen! Keep your wits about you and look after that violin. If it is stolen, all is lost."

"OK, but what about the fifth violin?"

"What?" said the Queen.

"Well, three of the top five are missing. I'm here with number four. Where is the fifth one?"

The Queen huffed. "The fifth one is in Cremona, Italy."

"Don't you think we should warn somebody, in case the thief steals that one tonight instead?"

"Ha!" said the Queen. "If you think I am going to call the President of Italy, you are mistaken. Why, just last week, at a pizza party, he told me that Italy has the finest museums in the world."

"OK...," I said.

"The nerve!" said the Queen. "You know what he meant! That his museums are better than mine! Poppycock!"

"Poppycock?"

"Balderdash!"

"Balderdash?"

"Rubbish!"

"OK," I said. "I get it now. I think."

"Your job is to keep this violin in Britain," said the Queen. "Now do your job. Good-bye!"

54

She hung up the phone.

"OK," I said.

I started walking back to the Messiah.

I heard a noise.

Oh no!

A thud!

The Messiah!

I ran to the gallery to make sure it was still there!

It was still there.

"Phew," I said.

But I knew I had heard a noise.

At least I thought I had heard a noise.

Had I really heard a noise?

I stood in the gallery, totally still, and listened.

Nothing.

It was very quiet.

I thought about what the Queen had said. When things are very quiet, that is how you know something exciting is going to happen. Suddenly, everything in the museum looked creepy.

The mummy cases looked creepy.

The samurai suit looked creepy.

The painting of the naked baby playing the violin looked creepy, but it had kind of always looked creepy.

(Now the dodo looked pretty creepy though!)

It was too quiet. I tried humming, but even my humming sounded creepy. So I pulled out my Walkman. In the 1980s, this is how we listened to music:

Today, when I am writing this book, this is how we listen to music:

If you are reading this book in the future, maybe you listen to music this way:

But in 1989, we listened to music on cassette tapes. It was the most advanced, highest quality way to hear a song.

But a lot of the time, the black tape came loose and unspooled from the tape.

"Aw man," I said. "It must have gotten shaken around in my bag."

I put my finger in one of the wheels on the front of the cassette and reeled the tape back in. I was pretty good at it. I had to do it on all my tapes and all my mom's tapes too, because when I was a kid I had little fingers.

When I was done, I put my New Kids on the Block tape in my Walkman and fast forwarded to the song I liked best.

"Much better," I said.

I continued my patrol.

Now everything in the museum looked really fun and cool.

But then, over the music, I heard another thud!

The thud was loud and close.
I ducked and hid behind a statue of a ram.

I pressed pause on my Walkman.
It was coming from the next gallery.
Thud! Thud! Thud!
Was somebody trying to tunnel up and bust
through the floor?
Was somebody trying to break down the wall?
Was somebody trying to jackhammer through the
ceiling?
I waited and watched.
What I saw made me gasp!

The lid of one of the mummy cases was moving!

Thud! Thud! Thud!

The top of the case was popping up, like someone was trying to get out.

Or some*thing*.

Some*thing* that used to be some*one*!

Thud! Thud! Thud!

Finally, the big stone lid became ajar.

The mummy case was open.

"No," I said to myself. "No."

Yes!

Slowly, a mummy rose up from the dark.

It grasped the side of the case and stepped out, putting one foot on the floor, then the other.

Its movements were slow and clumsy.

The mummy stood in the gallery and cracked its neck.

It looked around.

And then, the mummy started to walk.

I don't want to tell you what I did next.
But I will tell you.
I cried.

As quietly as I could, I cried.
I had never been so scared.
The mummy shambled toward me.
"No," I thought. "No no no no no no."
I curled up in a tiny ball behind the ram.
There was nowhere to run.
What would happen if the mummy caught me?
Would the mummy's touch put a curse on me?
That seemed like the best-case scenario.
I did not even want to think about the worst case.
The mummy was near me now.
I clenched my jaw and held my breath.

The mummy walked right by me.

It walked right by me!

I unclenched my jaw.

I took a breath.

(I was still crying, but now they were tears of joy.)

The mummy hadn't looked my way. It hadn't even known I was there.

But wait: If the mummy hadn't been coming to lay its curse on me, where was it going?

I rose to my knees and peered around a corner.

"Aw man," I said.

The mummy was standing in front of the Messiah. It was using a handheld laser to cut a hole in the case.

The laser's red beam traced a perfect circle in the glass.

The mummy reached out and popped the circle out from the case. Then it stuck its arm through the hole and gripped the violin by the neck. The mummy pulled the Messiah free.

The moon shone down through a high window. The mummy raised the violin above its head and laughed. Loose bandages hung off its body.

It was intense.

I sighed.

Curse or no curse, my job was to protect that violin. It was time to do my job.

"Halt!" I shouted.

The mummy stopped laughing and looked my way.

I was sprinting right toward it.

"Stop in the name of the law!" I said.

(I was kind of making stuff up at this point.)

The mummy turned and ran.

"Drop that violin!" I shouted.

"Actually, sorry!" I shouted. "Please do not drop it. It's very valuable. Gently place that violin down on the ground!"

It was hard to shout while I was running so fast.

I was gaining on the mummy.

"Actually, don't place the violin down on the ground either!" I shouted. "It might get dirty. Turn around and put it back in the case!"

The mummy was making a beeline for the museum's front door.

But the doors were locked.

The mummy was trapped.

"Ha!" I said. "I've got you now!"

The mummy picked up a chair from the café and threw it through a window.

There was a terrible crash. Shards flew everywhere. An alarm started to blare.

I ran forward and lunged for the mummy.

"Got you!" I said. I grabbed a loose bandage on the mummy's left leg.

But the mummy leaped through the window, and the bandage tore free.

I looked out the window. Glass crunched beneath my feet.

The mummy somersaulted across the pavement and hopped into a sports car.

The car's engine roared. The mummy drove off, its bandages trailing behind it like streamers on a bike's handlebars.

I looked down at the bandage in my hand. It was a perfect four-inch square.

"Aw man," I said. "Toilet paper."

"Oh dear," said the Queen of England.

"You keep saying that," I said.

I was speaking to her from a big red phone booth outside the museum.

"I keep thinking that," said the Queen. She sighed. "Oh dear."

The police had arrived and were searching the museum. The curator was there too.

"How dreadful," said the Queen of England. "Both violins missing."

"*Four* violins missing," I said.

"Well, I mainly care about two of them," said the Queen. "Mine."

"Hmmm," I said.

"And the only suspect is a mummy," said the Queen. "Perhaps I should call up Dracula and ask him whether he knows anything about this."

"It wasn't an actual mummy," I said.

"Thank you," said the Queen. "I am aware."

"The robber just wrapped himself up in toilet paper," I said.

"Please," said the Queen of England, "stop talking to me about toilet paper."

"OK," I said.

"Agent One," said the Queen, "I have some very bad news: You have failed at your mission. Leave this case to the police. Perhaps they will turn up a clue."

"They won't," I said.

"And how do you know?"

"Because," I said, "I already searched the museum

for clues."

"I see," said the Queen. "Well, that is even worse news. I am afraid there is nothing left for you to do but return home."

"No, but listen!" I said. "I searched the museum. And I found a clue."

"Well this is wonderful news!" said the Queen. "What did you find?"

"After the thief drove off in a Lamborghini, I peeked inside the mummy's coffin, where he'd been hiding. And guess what I found."

"A mummy!" said the Queen.

"No," I said.

"I am tired of guessing," said the Queen.

"I found a suit jacket," I said. "And there was a passport inside."

"This is an excellent clue!" said the Queen. "What does the passport say?"

"It's kind of hard to read," I said. "It's in Italian."

"Italian!" cried the Queen of England. "I knew it! I knew it! I knew it!"

"And that's not all," I said. "The suit jacket has a label from a tailor. And guess where that tailor shop is located?"

"I told you," said the Queen, "I am tired of guessing!"

"Cremona!"

The Queen screamed. "I knew it! Mac, look at the photograph in the passport. Is the man it belongs to quite dashing?"

I studied the photo.

"Um," I said. "He has an earring!"

"How very dashing!" said the Queen. "Don't you see? The President of Italy has sent a dashing spy around the world to steal Stradivarius violins!"

"Why would he do that?" I asked.

"Why indeed!" said the Queen. "I told you he is always boasting about his museums. Now the five finest Strads will all be in one place: Cremona, the birthplace of Antonio Stradivari! Oh, I will never hear the end of it. Mac, you must go to Cremona and retrieve those violins so I am spared the President's bragging!"

"And so they can be returned to their owners," I said.

"Oh, yes," said the Queen. "Right, that too. Good-bye."

She hung up.

Five seconds later, the phone rang.

"Hello?" I said.

"Hullo!" said the Queen. "May I speak to Mac? He is a very short American boy who is probably standing nearby."

"Speaking," I said.

"Agent One!" said the Queen. "I forgot to tell you. Do not be too hard on yourself about freezing up back there in the museum. It is hard to be alone, and even harder to be alone with a mummy."

"Thank you," I said.

"Even if that mummy turns out to just be a man who wrapped himself in toilet paper," said the Queen.

"OK," I said.

"And so," said the Queen of England, "I have sent you a little company."

There was a scratching at the door of the phone booth.

I looked out, and nobody was there.

So I looked down, and saw a short, long dog.

"Freddie!" I said. I opened the door and let him in. He jumped into my arms and licked my nose. I didn't mind.

"Now get to Italy and fetch those violins!" said the Queen. "Good-bye!"

19
ZIP
LINE

There is a tower in Cremona. It is called Torrazzo di Cremona, which is Italian for the "Tower of Cremona."

(Good name.)

The tower is more than seven hundred years old and almost 370 feet tall. It's the third tallest brickwork bell tower in the world!

(That's true. You can look it up, but why would I lie about something like that?)

There is a big clock on the front of the tower. But instead of just saying what time it is, this clock tells you what the moon is doing, and what zodiac sign is behind the sun.

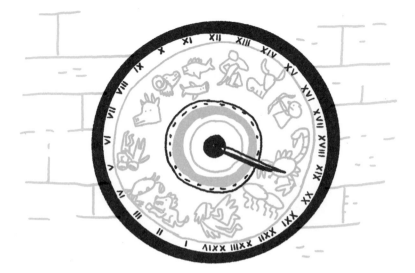

At dawn, I stood high in the spire of the Torrazzo, looking out through binoculars. It was scorpion o'clock.

Across the plaza, there was a low building topped with teeth-like parapets. It looked like an ancient fortress.

"The old town hall," I whispered to Freddie. "That's where they keep the Strads."

Freddie didn't care. He was licking the ground.

Behind those stone walls were millions of dollars worth of violins.

The plaza was empty. The old town hall was quiet. But I knew there would be guards by the entrances.

And that's why I wasn't going in through an entrance.

"Look out, Freddie," I said.

He kept licking the ground.

I pulled out a grappling hook from my backpack.

The hook was attached to a long cord coiled at my feet. I held on to the cord and swung the hook around and around in a wide circle.

"I hope this works," I said.

I winced and released my grip.

The grappling hook sailed over the town square, its cord trailing behind like a mummy's bandage.

It landed on the roof with a far-off clink.

"Yes!" I said.

Freddie kept licking the same spot. I think someone had dropped an ice cream there the night before.

It was nice having someone to talk to.

I gently pulled back on the cord. The hook slid across the roof and caught on the parapet.

"OK," I said. There was a metal pulley on the cord. I attached it to my belt while I hummed to myself.

DUM DOO DOO DUM
DOO DOO DUM
DOO DOO DUM
DOO DOO DUM
DOO DUM DUM
DOO DOO DUM

"Let's go, Freddie," I said. He took one last lick and jumped into my arms.

"On the count of three," I said.

I counted to three.

I was a little nervous, so I decided to count to ten.

"Eleven," I said, because I was still nervous.

Then I pushed off from the tower.

Freddie and I zipped down the cord.

I looked down at the plaza, which glowed in the rosy dawn light.

It was wonderful.

We landed with a small thud on the roof of the old town hall. Some clay tiles cracked beneath our weight. We did it!

There was a little door on the roof, a few feet away.

"Here's a spy tip, Freddie," I said. "If you want to break in somewhere, enter through an exit."

I unclipped the pulley from my belt and returned the spy gear to my backpack.

"All right." I nodded toward the door. "Let's move."

Just then, someone clapped a hand on my shoulder from behind me.

"*Alt!*" someone commanded in a loud voice. "That is Italian for 'halt'!"

"I figured," I said.

I sat in a pink room. A scowling guard stood in the corner.

He looked familiar, but I couldn't figure out how I knew him.

I was wearing handcuffs.

Freddie was tied to the wall on his leash.

The door opened, and a man in a nice suit walked into the room. He was carrying a plate.

"*Buongiorno*," he said.

It was the President of Italy.

FRANCESCO COSSIGA

He put the plate down on the table in front of me.

"We have some questions for you," said the President. "But first, eat."

There was a sandwich on the plate. It was shaped like a triangle and stuffed with meat.

I sniffed the sandwich. "What's in here? Truth juice?"

The President frowned. "Truth juice?"

"Yeah," I said. "Is it laced with some potion or serum that makes me spill my guts?"

The President winced.

"It's an expression," I said. "It means tell you everything I know."

"No," said the President. "There is no truth juice. Only prosciutto, artichokes, and mayonnaise."

"So a ham sandwich," I said.

The President smiled. "Yes. A ham sandwich."

I stared at the ham sandwich.

Even though the sandwich was tiny, I picked it up with both hands, because of the handcuffs.

I took a nibble.

"*What* is in here?" I said.

It was the best sandwich I'd ever eaten.

"Good?" the President asked.

"Yes!" I said. "Why is it so good?"

"Because," said the President, "it is made with the best ingredients. The best prosciutto, the best artichokes, the best eggs in the mayonnaise. A ham sandwich is a very good sandwich. But if you make it with the very best ingredients in the world, then it would be the *perfect version* of a ham sandwich."

"A ham sandwich that is even better than a ham sandwich," I said.

I finished the sandwich in two quick bites.

"You enjoyed it!" The President was delighted.

"I will remember this sandwich my whole life," I said.

(So far, I have.)

"Can I have another?" I asked.

"Of course!" The President stopped smiling and pulled the plate back toward himself. "But not until you answer some questions."

I slumped in my chair. I would have crossed my arms against my chest, if it weren't for the handcuffs.

"I see what's going on here," I said.

When you could make a sandwich that good, you didn't need truth juice.

"That's right." The President leaned forward. "It is time to spill your guts."

22

QUESTIONS
AND
ANSWERS

"Who do you work for?" the President asked.

I shook my head. "Sorry, not talking."

"Please," said the President. "This will go better for everyone, yourself included, if you answer my questions."

"This isn't fair," I said. "*I* should be the one asking *you* the questions."

"Ha!" said the President. "What you say is ridiculous! You want to ask me questions? I am the President! You are a violin thief!"

"I know you are, but what am I?" I said.

The President looked puzzled. "What?"

"It's an expression," I said. "We say it at school."

"What does it mean?"

"It means *you're* a violin thief," I said.

"You are!" said the President.

"Nuh-uh," I said. "You are."

"Outrageous!" said the President. "You came here to steal the Cremonese, our finest violin!"

"No!" I said. "I came here to steal back the violins you stole!"

"What?" he said.

"Yes!" I said.

"Wait," he said.

"The tables have turned!" I said.

"Please," said the President. "Quiet down. What you are saying makes no sense. We know you are here to steal our most treasured violin, the Cremonese."

"Prove it," I said.

The President smiled. "I will! Yesterday I got a phone call from a mysterious man, warning me that a short boy with a short dog was going to try to steal the Cremonese."

"That's a lie!" I said.

The only person who knew I was on this mission was the Queen of England.

"Why would I lie?" asked the President.

"Because," I said, "you are a thief!"

"Allow me to use an expression: I know that is something true about you, but in that case who am I?" said the President. "Did I get that right?"

"No," I said.

"Oh well," said the President. "Explain this: Last week, this museum's guard had his coat stolen."

Over in the corner, the guard was really scowling now.

"His passport was in one of his pockets. And now, in your knapsack, we find this."

He placed my backpack on the table, unzipped it, and took out the suit jacket I'd found in the museum.

I looked up at the guard. "That's where I know you from! I didn't recognize you without your earring!"

"The President does not think I should wear it at work," said the guard.

"Well, the Queen of England thinks it's dashing," I said.

The guard blushed.

The President pounded the table.

"Aha!" said the President. "I have tricked you into answering my question. You work for the Queen of England. Of course she wanted to steal my violin. She is always bragging that her country has the best museums in the world."

"But that's what she says about—" I didn't finish my sentence. Sometimes my mom and dad had me pass messages to each other, and it never went well. I had a feeling I was caught in the middle here too, and it was time to get out.

"Look," I said. "I didn't steal that suit coat. A mummy did."

"That," said the President, "is probably the worst excuse I have ever heard."

"Let me explain," I said. And I did. I told him all about the missing violins and the mummy and my mission.

When I was done, the President frowned. "You seem like you are telling the truth, but your story is very strange. Why would somebody call and tell me you were coming to steal my violin?"

"Someone wanted to make it seem like I was the thief."

"But who would do such a thing?" said the President. "And why? I do not have the stolen violins, and you do not want to steal my violin, so what are we all doing here, in this room?"

I had a terrible realization.

"If the guard is guarding me," I said, "who is guarding your violin?"

The President turned pale.

So did the guard.

I probably did too.

Freddie just stood there wagging his tail though.

"Yoo-hoo!" Outside, somebody was shouting.

The President and I ran to the window.

There was a man wearing blue jeans standing down in the plaza, holding a violin above his head.

It was the KGB Man.

"The Cremonese!" said the President. "He stole our violin!"

"Give it back!" I shouted. "Or I'll make you regret it!"

The KGB Man grinned. "That is a ridiculous thing for someone wearing handcuffs to say! You are ridiculous!"

"I promise, I will come for you!" I shouted. "I will get those violins!"

"But how will you get the violin," said the KGB Man, "if you are wearing those handcuffs?" He laughed harder.

"You do not deserve to touch a Stradivarius!" shouted the President.

"Do not worry, Mr. President!" said the KGB Man. "These violins are going to good hands, the hands of the finest musicians in the world!"

He opened the trunk of his sports car and put the violin inside.

He hopped behind the steering wheel and waved up at us.

"*Dasvidaniya! Arrivederci!* Good-bye! Oh, I am sorry! I forgot that you cannot wave back, because of your handcuffs!"

The KGB Man peeled away.

"Those were nice jeans," said the President of Italy.

"Could you take off these handcuffs?" I said.

"Well, this is going terribly!" said the Queen of England.

"Yeah," I said.

I'd called her from a phone booth to update her on my mission.

"I must say," said the Queen, "this news puts me in a foul mood. Rather, it keeps me in a foul mood, because I began the day in a foul mood, because that infernal song you were humming the other day is *still* stuck in my head."

"Oh yeah," I said. "The Tetris song. It's really catchy."

"It is driving me to distraction!" said the Queen.

"Sorry," I said. "Hey! You should listen to that New Kids on the Block song I told you about! 'The Right Stuff'! It might knock the Tetris song out of your head!"

"I refuse to," said the Queen of England. "I do not think I will like it, and I do not want to speak about it again."

"OK," I said. "But what should I do about the KGB Man?"

"Find him," said the Queen of England, "and get those two violins back."

"*Five* violins," I said. "Now he has the five best violins in the world."

"Yes, yes," said the Queen. "If you're able to, of course get all five violins! But make sure you get the two British ones especially!"

"Hmmm," I said.

"Oh, don't give me that 'hmmm,'" said the Queen.

"Your Majesty," I asked, "who are the finest musicians in the world?"

"That's easy," said the Queen of England. "The Royal Philharmonic Orchestra. They are right here in London. Why do you ask?"

"Because," I said, "it's the only clue I've got. The KGB Man said he was taking the violins to the finest musicians in the world. If I find those musicians, maybe I'll find the violins."

"That doesn't make any sense," said the Queen of England. "Why would he steal violins from Britain, just to bring them back here? Of course, if he brought all five violins here, that would be very interesting . . . After all, we do have the finest musicians in the world."

I decided to ask a different question. "Your Majesty, who would a *Russian* say are the finest musicians in the world?"

"Oh," said the Queen. "That is a different matter entirely."

This is the Red Army Choir.

Their official name was A. V. Alexandrov Twice Red-Bannered and Red-Starred Academic Song and Dance Ensemble of the Soviet Army.

(Now that's a name.)

The Red Army Choir was the official military choir of the USSR.

The musicians in the Red Army Choir all performed while wearing their military uniforms.

Which is why, on one cold Russian day in 1989, I was dressed like this:

I had flown to Leningrad, in the USSR.

Today, Leningrad is called Saint Petersburg.

Most of the country that was the USSR is called Russia.

Today, the A. V. Alexandrov Twice Red-Bannered and Red-Starred Academic Song and Dance Ensemble of the Soviet Army is just called the Alexandrov Ensemble. But mostly people still call it the Red Army Choir.

I was standing outside a big cathedral, wearing a Soviet Army uniform made for me by a tailor in Cremona. I milled about with other musicians. I tried not to make eye contact, so that nobody would talk to me.

I was undercover as a Russian musician.

I did not speak Russian.

I did not play any musical instruments.

This was a risky mission.

Luckily, Freddie was stuffed down the front of my shirt.

Having him there helped me feel less scared.

Also, Leningrad is chilly, and Freddie was warm.

Somebody blew a horn.

The musicians snapped to attention.

I did too.

Somebody shouted out a command in Russian.

The musicians began marching toward the church.

I did too.

"Here we go, Freddie," I said.

25
WITH THE
BAND

The Red Army Choir was arranged in rows in the front of the cathedral.

I stood between two tall soldiers with flutes.

I took out my recorder.

My plan in Leningrad was to do the same thing I did at the school concerts: pretend to play the recorder and smile.

I scanned the orchestra.

There were musical instruments I had never seen before:

a balalaika,

a domra,

and a bayan.

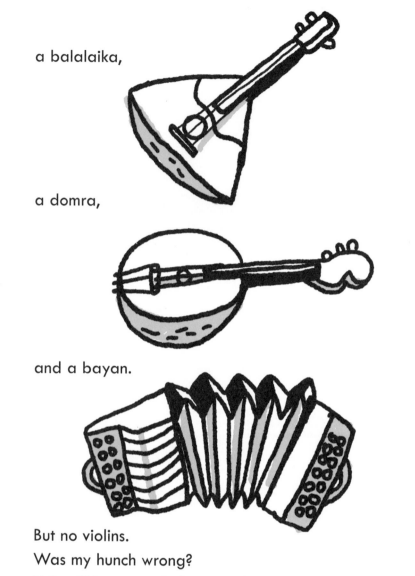

But no violins.

Was my hunch wrong?

What if I got caught here, and it was all for nothing?

My hands started to sweat.

The orchestra warmed up.

A conductor came out and tapped his baton on a music stand.

I thought about faking like I was about to throw up
and running out of the church.

And then a door opened and six people came out.

Five of them were holding violins.

The sixth was the KGB Man.

The Strads! They were here!

The KGB Man stood next to the conductor and began speaking in Russian.

The only word I could understand was "Stradivarius." At one point, he said something, and all the musicians laughed.

"Ha, ha, ha!" I said, and smiled at the flutist on my right.

He smiled back.

When the KGB Man finished talking, everybody— the conductor, the musicians, the KGB Man—reached into their pockets and pulled out earplugs.

They put the earplugs in their ears.

What in the world was going on?

I started to panic.

I patted my pockets even though I knew I didn't have any earplugs on me. I could feel Freddie squirming under my jacket.

The flutist elbowed me sharply. I looked over at him. He was holding out an extra pair.

He said something to me in Russian and smiled.

"Ha, ha, ha!" I said. I took the earplugs and put them in my ears.

The conductor raised his baton.

The musicians raised their instruments.

I held my recorder in my sweaty hands.

Everything was silent. Not a silence I could hear, because I was wearing earplugs.

A silence I could *feel*.

The orchestra began to play.

The Red Army Choir was famous for its discipline.

Sometimes, in the middle of the performance, the conductor would walk out of the room, and the musicians would continue to play in perfect unison.

That is pretty impressive.

But the day I was there they played a song without even hearing what they were playing.

It was *very* impressive.

I put the recorder up to my mouth and pretended to blow into it.

Every so often I would pause and smile.

The five violinists stood at the very front of the orchestra, furiously playing the Strads.

We played for five minutes, and then, all at once, everyone stopped.

The KGB Man took out his earplugs and stood up in his pew. "Bravo!" he shouted. "Bravo!"

The conductor bowed to him.

The soldiers in the orchestra all looked straight ahead.

The whole thing was weird.

The KGB Man started to speak Russian again. While he talked, my mind raced. I eyed the soldiers holding the Strads. I wondered how many of them I could overpower.

Probably zero.

I would have to use my wits to get those violins back.

The KGB Man made another joke, and everyone laughed.

"Ha, ha, ha!" I said.

The flutist did not look at me.

And then, at the end of a very long sentence, the KGB Man clapped his hands together once, and everyone in the orchestra sat down on the floor at the same time.

Everyone, that is, except me.

The KGB Man smiled. "Hello, Mac."

"Perhaps," said the KGB Man, "you are wondering what I was just saying. I will translate for you: 'Thank you, comrades, for your wonderful music. It will serve our country well in our fight against the West! And I have noticed that we have a surprise guest: a secret agent for the Queen of England! Of course, he cannot understand a word I am saying, because he does not speak Russian! So let us play a little joke on him, yes? When I clap my hands, please, comrades, sit down on the ground, all at the same time!'"

"Aw man," I said.

"But, Mac," said the KGB Man, "you look different from the last time I saw you. You were wearing something else . . ."

"Yeah," I said. "I was just wearing my regular clothes, but now I'm in a disguise."

"No, that is not it . . ."

The KGB Man frowned and stared at me, then brightened up. "Oh yes, now I know what you are missing. These!"

He removed a pair of handcuffs from his jacket pocket and laughed.

"Ha ha ha ha ha ha ha ha!"

"You shouldn't laugh at your own jokes," I said. "It's not cool."

"That is a silly rule," said the KGB Man. "And besides, my joke was so funny! Ha ha ha ha ha ha ha ha! Hold on, I want to tell everybody what I just said, and then what you just said, and then what I just said."

He switched back to Russian. I could tell when he was doing an impression of me. When he finished talking, the whole Red Army Choir laughed.

"Mac, I wish you spoke Russian," said the KGB Man, "because it is even funnier in Russian!"

Finally he collected himself. "Please come up here and put on these handcuffs."

"OK."

I made my way down through the orchestra, to the floor of the cathedral.

My footsteps echoed off the walls.

The KGB Man smirked at me as I approached.

I held out my wrists in front of myself.

Then I smiled and shouted, "Psych!"

The KGB Man's smirk vanished.

I faked left, then ran to his right. He tried to grab me, but I was too fast.

The Red Army Choir rose to its feet and streamed down the risers.

"*Poymay yego!*" the KGB Man shouted. "That means 'seize him'!"

"I figured!" I said. Then I dove across the shiny marble floor, under a pew.

The noise was terrible.

The cathedral was filled with stomping and shouting.

I crawled from pew to pew, trying to stay small.

The orchestra poured into the nave of the cathedral while the KGB Man shouted commands.

The strings spread out along the southern wall.

The brass section covered the north.

The percussionists pounded down the center aisle, beating their drums as they marched.

The choir stayed put and began to chant a deep and rumbling song.

It was terrifying.

I peeked out from behind my pew.

"One, two, three," I whispered. I scrambled to the next row.

But as I was in the open, a drummer cried out.

Soldiers rushed toward me, grasping.

They were everywhere!

I climbed on top of the pew and hopped into the next row. I ran toward some columns that could give me cover.

A grimacing Soviet with a huge scar on his face blocked my path.

I turned to flee in the other direction, but three men holding trumpets were slowly advancing toward me.

The man with the scar laughed and lunged at me with giant hands.

Freddie popped out of the front of my shirt and growled.

The big man stopped. His eyes got huge. I must have looked like some two-headed monster!

While he was standing there startled, I slid right between his legs.

I rounded a column and came face to face with another soldier.

He swung a balalaika at my head—at my heads!—but I ducked. The instrument made an awful song as it shattered against the stone pillar.

Freddie hopped out of the front of my shirt. He tugged at the man's pant cuff with his teeth, which gave me the chance to escape. I sprinted for the exit, dodging soldiers. Saints frowned at me from portraits in gilt frames on the wall.

I made it to the cathedral's huge wooden doors.

Freddie was holding off a small group of trumpeters, growling and baring his teeth.

"Come on, Freddie!" I cried. "Let's go!"

He turned and ran to me, his big tongue lolling. I clapped my hands and he jumped into my arms. I gave him a big pat and told him he was a good dog.

I took one last look back at the cathedral. The orchestra was in disarray. The percussionists were stumbling forward. Scattered string players were pointing their fingers and shouting. The brass section shook their fists.

I smiled and pushed through the cathedral's huge doors.

Cold air blasted my face. I was outside.

"Aw man," I said.

A line of men holding piccolos, oboes, and clarinets stood in the gray afternoon, blocking my way. The KGB Man was there too, twirling his handcuffs. He was smirking again. "You forgot about the woodwinds."

My old friend the flutist swept me up in a big bear hug. He lifted me off my feet.

The KGB Man slapped the handcuffs on my wrists.
"And now," said the KGB Man, "you are a prisoner
of the Soviet Union."

Freddie and I were taken to a Soviet jail.

The KGB Man locked us in a tiny cell.

The walls were cracked and windowless. The floor was so cold I could feel it through my sneakers. There was a small cot in the corner. It did not have sheets, or even a pillow.

On the other side of the bars, the KGB Man smirked.

"I am sorry," he said. "You have lost, Mac."

I stared back at him and said, "Call me Agent One."

"Ha!" said the KGB Man. "Agent One. That is dumb. I like it!"

I shrugged.

"I am afraid this is the end of our long history," said the KGB Man. "It has been fun going head to head with you. But my head is better." He tapped his temple.

"OK," I said.

"I will miss you, Agent One!" said the KGB Man. "Maybe I will come visit you, once my plan is done!"

My head snapped up. "Aren't you finished? You have the violins. You can go put them in some Russian museum."

"A museum!" said the KGB Man. "I did not steal these violins to put them under glass in some marble building. A Stradivarius should be *played*! Such a wonderful tone! There is nothing like it in the world. Ah, I wish you could have heard them."

"Yeah," I said, "why did we all wear earplugs back there?"

"Do you know about the sirens, Agent One? From the Greek myths?"

"I like Greek myths!" I said.

(I still do.)

"Then you will like this," said the KGB Man. "The legend goes that the sirens were beautiful creatures who lived in the sea. The sound of their singing was so beautiful that it would drive sailors mad and make them crash their ships on the rocks."

"I don't think Strads could sound *that* good," I said.

"On their own, *nyet*," said the KGB Man. "But when playing the right song . . ." He smiled. "I think you know it!"

He cleared his throat, and he began to sing.

I had no idea what he was saying, because I don't speak Russian.

But I recognized the tune.

dum doo doo dum

doo doo dum

doo doo dum

doo doo dum

doo dum dum doo doo dum

"The Tetris song!" I cried. "I didn't know it had words."

The KGB Man nodded. "They are very sad words."

"The Tetris song is sad?"

The KGB Man shrugged. "Most Russian songs are sad."

"The Tetris song is *Russian*?"

"Agent One," said the KGB Man, "*Tetris* is Russian."

"What are you talking about?" I asked.

He opened my cell door and tossed me my backpack.

Before I could escape, he locked it again.

"Please," said the KGB Man, "take out the game."

I pulled out the box that held my copy of Tetris.

I gasped!

31

FROM RUSSIA
WITH FUN!

I had never really looked at the box before:

"'From Russia with fun'?" I said.

"Yes!" said the KGB Man. "It is a joke about a book with James Bond. *'From Russia with Love'*! There is a movie too. Have you seen it?"

"No," I said. "Too much romance."

I still couldn't believe it. Tetris comes from Russia.

"Ah," the KGB Man nodded gravely. "I will tell you a story. In 1984, in Moscow, a scientist named Alexey was working on a secret project for the Soviet Union: a computer that could think! To test his thinking computer, he invented a game for it to play. A game where blocks fell from the sky, and you had to arrange them into lines."

"Tetris," I said.

"*Da,*" said the KGB Man. "Tetris! Well, forget about the thinking computer. Humans loved Tetris. Other scientists in the lab started playing, and soon scientists at other labs. And this is when the Soviet Union knew: We owned something special."

"What do you mean the Soviet Union owns it?" I said. "Alexey made it."

"Of course," said the KGB Man. "And he is a scientist for the Soviet Union, using computers that belong to a Soviet Union lab. We own what he made."

"Hmmm," I said.

"Everyone in the world wanted Tetris," said the KGB Man. "The British. The Americans. The Japanese. You have heard of Nintendo?" said the KGB Man.

I sighed. "You know I've heard of Nintendo," I said.

"Nintendo, they paid the Soviet Union a lot of money so that they could give away a copy of Tetris with every Game Boy in America! A *lot* of money. How wonderful!"

"Wait," I said. "Is this true?"

"You can look it up," said the KGB Man. "But here is something even more wonderful than all that money. Now, Tetris, it needed a good song while you played the game. And so they used 'Korobeiniki,' a very old and sad Russian song."

"The Tetris song," I said.

"*Da*," said the KGB Man. "Now, at KGB, we noticed something interesting. American children, they were always humming 'Korobeiniki.'"

"It's catchy," I said.

"I think," said the KGB Man, "it is the catchiest song of all time."

"I agree," I said. "It really gets stuck in your head."

"Exactly!" said the KGB Man. "Stuck in your head. I love this expression."

"OK," I said.

"You see, at this time, I was reminded of another Greek myth. The Trojan horse! The Greeks, they were at war with Troy. And to win this war, they played a trick. They made a big, beautiful horse. And then a bunch of soldiers climbed inside the horse and hid. The Greeks rolled their horse up to the walls of Troy. 'Yoo-hoo!' they said. 'We would like to give you a gift!' And the Trojans loved this beautiful horse, and they wheeled it into their city. Once the horse was inside the gate, all the soldiers hopped out, and the Greeks won the war!"

"OK . . . ," I said.

"Don't you see?" said the KGB Man. "Tetris is the siren Trojan Horse! You welcomed it into your countries, and we stuck our song in your brains!"

I did not like where this was going.

"And then," said the KGB Man, "I had an idea."

He tapped his temple. "You know, Agent One, that the Cold War is fought not with soldiers, but in our minds."

"I know," I said.

His voice dropped to a whisper. "What if I got

'Korobeiniki' stuck in someone's head *forever?* She would be distracted. She would be annoyed! She would be easier to outsmart."

"She?" I asked. But I knew who he meant.

"The Queen of England," said the KGB Man. "But to really get it stuck, in the worst kind of way, I would need something special. 'Korobeiniki' is a very good song. But what if I made it with the very best instruments in the world? Then it would be the *perfect version* of the song."

"Like a ham sandwich that's even better than a ham sand-wich," I said.

The KGB Man frowned. "What?"

"You'll never succeed!" I cried.

"I already have!" He pulled a cassette tape from his pocket and shook it in the air. "'Korobeiniki,' recorded by the Red Army Choir, on the five finest Stradivarius violins!"

When the KGB Man shook the cassette, the black tape came loose. "I hate it when that happens," he said.

"Yeah," I said. "Me too."

He tried to turn the spool back with his pointer finger, but it was too big.

His face got red. "My finger is too fat! No! This wheel is too small." He looked up at me. "You have tiny child hands. Help me."

I scoffed. "Why would I help you with your evil plan?"

"Because." The KGB Man grinned. "If you help me, I will take off your handcuffs."

I thought for a second. "OK," I said.

He passed me the cassette.

I twisted my finger and reeled the tape back in.

The KGB Man strutted in front of my cage.

He was feeling pleased with himself.

"It really is wonderful," said the KGB Man. "For years, you have been polluting our brains with your songs. The Beatles. Bruce Springsteen. And now these New Kids on the Block. Garbage."

"That one New Kids song is actually pretty good," I said. "'The Right Stuff.' I keep trying to get the Queen of England to listen to it, but she won't."

The KGB Man stopped strutting. "She is stubborn," he said. He held out his hand.

"Here you go," I said.

He took the cassette from me.

"Thank you," said the KGB Man. "I will be sure to tell her you helped."

Through the bars, he unlocked my cuffs.

"She'll love that," I said.

I rubbed my wrists.

"Hey," I said. "Why did you tell me all this?"

"I wanted you to know!" The KGB Man was delighted. "And you cannot stop me. There is no escaping from Soviet spy jail!"

He strolled away, chuckling.

When I knew he was gone, I kicked the door.

I rattled my bars.

A guard came by and glared at me.

The KGB Man was right.

There was no escaping from Soviet spy jail.

I lay down on the cot.

Freddie hopped up with me. He let me use him as a pillow.

"I am glad you are here, Freddie," I said.

I closed my eyes, but I was too worried to sleep.

The next morning, a spy snuck onto the grounds of Buckingham Palace.

He was wearing a tan trench coat, sunglasses, and a big hat.

He crept up to the side of the castle and called out, "Yoo-hoo!"

Three floors up, the Queen of England put down the book she'd just started. (She had finished the last one. She'd finally gotten the Tetris song out of her head.)

The Queen opened her window and looked down at the lawn.

The spy tore off his sunglasses and flung his hat into some shrubs. He unbuttoned his coat, because he'd been hiding something inside it.

It was a boom box.

A boom box was a box with speakers that played music really loud.

(Good name.)

In the 1980s, we used boom boxes to blast out songs from tapes.

The spy's coat hung down loosely. He was wearing a white T-shirt and American blue jeans.

"Ugh," said the Queen of England. "It's you."

"Yes," said the KGB Man, "it's me. I have something I want you to hear."

The Queen of England sighed.

The KGB Man placed earplugs inside his ears. He pressed play on the boom box and raised it above his head.

The song began.

The Queen of England looked bored.

The KGB Man's eyes grew wide.

The Queen of England rolled hers.

Frenzied, the KGB Man tore out his earplugs.

"What is this?" he asked.

It was five American singers—the nice one, the cute one, the shy one, the older brother, and the bad boy—singing their big hit.

"Oh oh oh oh oh
Oh oh oh oh
Oh oh oh oh oh
The right stuff!"

(It's really hard to write a great tune using only words. Just listen to it yourself. It's actually really good.)

The KGB Man was furious. He pressed stop on the boom box.

"That is the song Mac was talking about?" asked the Queen of England. She thought for a second, then tilted her head. "It was OK."

"He switched the tapes!" cried the KGB Man. "He switched the tapes!"

"I have no idea what you're talking about," said the Queen of England, "but I am certain you are not supposed to be here. Guards, place this man in hand-cuffs."

At least, that's how I heard it happened. The Queen told me about it later, and sometimes she exaggerated her stories. When everything in the last chapter went down, I was rotting away in a Soviet cell.

But I wouldn't be there for long.

During the Cold War, there was a thing called a prisoner exchange. A prisoner exchange would go like this: When the West captured a very important Soviet spy, the East would trade a very important spy with the Queen of England.

In 1989, the Soviet Union traded me for the KGB Man.

He got to leave British spy jail and go home.

And I got to leave Soviet spy jail and go home.

(Freddie also got to leave spy jail. I gave him a few pats and then he went home too.)

My mom was very happy to see me. I told her what I could about what I'd been up to, but I had to leave out a lot, because it was top secret, and besides, it would just make her worried.

The first thing I did was go up to sleep in my bed.

Dogs are OK for pillows, but they can be a little bit bony.

I pulled up the covers and curled into a ball.

But just as I was about to drift off, the phone rang.

It was the Queen of England.

"Hello," I said.

"Hullo!" she said. "May I speak to Mac?"

"Speaking," I said.

"Mac," said the Queen, "you sound tired."

"Mmm hmm," I said. "I was falling asleep."

"Before you even opened your present?" said the Queen. "I sent you a thank-you gift!"

I looked at my desk and saw a little red box.

I unwrapped it. Inside was a thick business card. It said:

AGENT ONE

"Wow," I said. "This is the nicest thing you've ever sent me."

The Queen of England frowned.

(I could tell she was frowning, even over the phone.)

"Well, that can't be true."

"Anyway, thanks," I said. "And thanks for trading the KGB Man to get me back. It made me feel really important!"

"I traded the KGB man to get you, five priceless violins, and an adorable corgi back," said the Queen of England. "Don't get full of yourself. It's unappealing."

"OK," I said.

"Now," said the Queen of England, "I have a favor to ask."

I smiled and said, "OK."

Mac Barnett is a *New York Times* bestselling author of children's books and a former ███████████. His books have received awards such as the Caldecott Honor, the E. B. White Read Aloud Award, and the Boston Globe-Horn Book Award. His secret agent work has received awards such as the Medal of ████████████, the Cross of ████████████, and the Royal Order of ████████████ ████████████ the Third. His favorite color is ████████. His favorite food is ████████. He lives in Oakland, California. (That's true. You can look it up.)

Mike Lowery used to get in trouble for doodling in his books, and now he's doing it for a living. His drawings have been in dozens of books for kids and adults, and on everything from greeting cards to food trucks. Mike is the author and illustrator of *Random Illustrated Facts*, and the books, *Everything Awesome About Dinosaurs and Other Prehistoric Beasts* and *Everything Awesome About Sharks and Other Underwater Creatures,* with more Everything Awesome series titles to come. Mike lives in Atlanta, Georgia, with a little German lady and two genius kids.